Disney
FROZEN
5-
MINUTE
STORIES

DISNEY PRESS
Los Angeles • New York

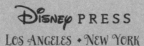

CONTENTS

FROZEN

The kingdom of Arendelle was a happy place. The king and queen had two young daughters, Anna and Elsa. The girls were their pride and joy. But the family had a secret. Elsa could create ice and snow with her hands.

One night, Anna convinced Elsa to turn the ballroom into a winter wonderland. As the sisters happily played together, Elsa accidentally lost control of her magic. An icy blast hit Anna in the head, and she fell to the floor, unconscious.

The king and queen rushed the girls to the trolls, mysterious healers who knew about magic. A wise troll named Grand Pabbie saved Anna by removing her memories of Elsa's magic. He explained that she was lucky to have been hit in the head, not in the heart.

The troll told the king and queen that Elsa's powers would only grow stronger. "Fear will be her enemy," he warned.

The king and queen knew they had to protect their daughter. To keep her magic a secret, they closed the kingdom's gates.

The king gave Elsa gloves to contain her powers, but the girl was still afraid she might hurt someone. She even avoided Anna to keep her safe.

Then, when Anna and Elsa were teenagers, their parents were lost at sea. The sisters had never felt more alone.

Elsa stayed inside, where she could hide her magic. But she could not keep the castle gates closed forever. On the day of her coronation, her subjects were invited inside to celebrate.

Anna was thrilled at the chance to meet new people! She had barely stepped outside when she met Prince Hans of the Southern Isles. The two instantly fell in love.

At the coronation ball, Prince Hans asked Anna to marry him. Anna said yes, and the couple went to ask Elsa for her blessing.

Elsa refused to bless the marriage. She couldn't let Anna marry a man she had just met!

Anna couldn't believe her sister. "Why do you shut me out? What are you so afraid of?" she cried.

As Elsa fought with her sister, she lost control of her magic. Ice shot out of her hands. Now all of Arendelle knew her secret.

Panicked, Elsa fled into the mountains.

With her secret out, Elsa let her powers loose. A storm raged around her as she created an ice palace and even changed the way she looked.

Below her, ice and snow covered Arendelle. Anna felt awful! Leaving Hans in charge, she went after her sister.

As Anna trekked through the forest, she lost her horse. Luckily, she met an ice harvester named Kristoff and his reindeer, Sven. The two agreed to help her find Elsa.

High in the mountains, Anna and Kristoff came across a
dazzling winter wonderland, where they met a living snowman!
"I'm Olaf," he said.

Anna realized that Elsa must have created him. She asked
Olaf to lead them to Elsa so she could bring back summer. Olaf
loved the idea of summer and happily led them to Elsa's palace.

Inside, Anna told Elsa about the terrible winter storm in Arendelle. "It's okay. You can just unfreeze it," she said.

But Elsa didn't know how to stop the snow. Frustrated, she cried out, "I can't!" An icy blast shot across the room and hit Anna in the heart!

Kristoff rushed to help Anna. "I think we should go," he said.

At the base of the mountain, Kristoff noticed that Anna's hair was turning white. He knew his friends the trolls could help.

Grand Pabbie saw at once that Anna was hurt. "There is ice in your heart, put there by your sister," he said. "If not removed, to solid ice you will freeze, forever."

Grand Pabbie explained that only an act of true love could thaw a frozen heart.

Anna knew Hans was her true love. Maybe a kiss from him would save her. Anna, Kristoff, Sven, and Olaf raced back to Arendelle to find him.

But Hans was not in Arendelle. He had set out to look for Anna when her horse returned without her.

Hans and the search party arrived at Elsa's palace. The men attacked Elsa, and she defended herself. Suddenly, one of the men aimed a crossbow at Elsa! Hans pushed it aside, and the arrow hit a chandelier. It crashed to the ground, knocking Elsa out.

Hans and his men took her back to Arendelle and threw her in the dungeon.

Outside the kingdom, Anna, Kristoff, Olaf, and Sven hurried down the mountain. Anna was getting weaker by the minute. Kristoff was worried about her.

At the castle gates, he passed her to the royal servants. He was starting to realize that he cared deeply about Anna, but he knew that her true love, Hans, could make her well again.

Anna found Hans in the library. She asked him to save her
life with a kiss, but he refused! Hans had only been pretending to
love Anna so that he could take over Arendelle.

Putting out the room's fire, he left Anna to freeze.

In the dungeon, all Elsa could think about was getting away from Arendelle. It was the only way to protect everyone from her powers. Elsa became so upset that she froze the whole dungeon and escaped!

Alone in the library, Anna realized how reckless she had been. In trying to find love, she had doomed herself and her sister.

Just when Anna had given up all hope, Olaf arrived. The snowman lit a fire, even though Anna worried that he might melt.

"Some people are worth melting for," he said.

Olaf looked out the window and saw Kristoff returning. The snowman realized that Kristoff was the true love who could save Anna!

Olaf helped Anna outside, where she spotted Kristoff across the frozen fjord. If she could reach him in time, she would be saved!

But then she saw something else: Hans was about to strike Elsa with his sword!

With her remaining strength, Anna threw herself in front of Elsa. Hans's sword came down just as Anna's body froze to solid ice.

Elsa wrapped her arms around her frozen sister. "Oh, Anna," she sobbed.

Then something amazing happened: Anna began to thaw!

"An act of true love will thaw a frozen heart," Olaf said, realizing what had happened.

"Love!" Elsa cried, looking at Anna. "That's it!" Elsa realized that love was the key to her magic. She reversed the winter and brought back summer.

Hans was astonished to see Anna alive. "Anna?" he said. "But she froze your heart."

"The only frozen heart around here is yours!" Anna said, and sent him reeling with one punch.

With summer restored, Arendelle returned to normal—but from then on, the castle gates were open for good. For the first time in a long while, Arendelle was a happy place again. And Queen Elsa and Princess Anna were the happiest of all, for they had found their way back to each other!

A Royal Sleepover

"Pssssst! Elsa?" Anna gently nudged her sister. "Wake up."

Elsa shifted, groggy. "Go to bed, Anna," she said.

"I can't sleep!" Anna flopped down on Elsa's bed. Then she smiled slyly. "Wanna have a sleepover?"

Elsa opened her eyes and grinned. That sounded like fun!

Anna went to her room to find extra pillows and blankets. Meanwhile, Elsa headed to the kitchen to get the ingredients for her famous honey cones. After all, a sleepover wasn't a sleepover without snacks!

When Elsa got back to her room, she found Anna digging through the closet. "Aha!" Anna cried. "I knew it was here!"

Anna held up an old, worn book. Her parents had read it to the sisters every night when they were little.

"Let's see, we've got books, games, and this face cream Oaken gave me the last time I went to the trading post," Anna said. She opened the cream. "It looks kinda . . . goopy."

Elsa laughed. "Let's save *that* for later!"

Elsa looked around. It had been a long time since she'd had a sleepover. "Sooo . . . what should we do first?" she asked.

Anna was ready. "How about we build a fort, like when we were kids?" she suggested.

Anna stacked pillows and blankets around the room, making lookouts and hidden caves. Meanwhile, Elsa created icy tunnels and snowy turrets.

"This is fun," Elsa said, putting the finishing touches on an icy archway. "I think we should add a—"

SMACK! Elsa felt something soft and feathery hit her back. She turned to see a fallen pillow and a giggling Anna.

"Oh, no you don't!" Elsa yelled, launching a snowball at her sister. Anna ducked, squealing in delight.

Before long, the room was covered
in snow flurries and feathers. Anna was
zooming down an icy slide on the fort
when there was a knock at the door.

"Is it daytime already?" a familiar
voice asked.

"Olaf!" Anna cried. The sisters
welcomed their snowman friend inside.
Elsa explained that they were having
a sleepover and invited Olaf to join
them.

"A sleepover?" Olaf asked,
excited. "Oh, I've always wanted
to have one of those." He
paused. "What's a
sleepover?"

"We'll show you," Anna said. "Come on! We were just about to play a game!"

Soon the friends were happily playing. Olaf was a natural at Pick-Up Sticks.

And Anna was great at Work of Art. She guessed every drawing and sculpture!

Charades proved to be a bit more challenging. Olaf twisted his body this way and that, making frantic gestures and grinning widely. The sisters didn't know what the answer could be. Finally, Elsa had an idea.

"Olaf, are you acting out 'summer'?" she asked.

"Yes!" he cried. "You're good at this!"

Elsa laughed. "Maybe it's time to do something else," she said. "How about a scary story?"

Anna went first, using her spookiest, most dramatic voice. "According to legend, the Hairy Hooligan only comes out on nights like these, looking for his next victim."

"How do you know when the Hairy Hooligan is around?" Olaf asked.

"He lets out a low moan," Anna answered.

"*OOOOOOOHHHHH.*" A sad whine echoed through the room.

"Wow. That's really scary, Anna," Olaf said, impressed.

"Uh . . ." Anna blinked. "That wasn't me."

"*OOOOOOOOOHHHHHH!*" The cry sounded like it was coming from outside the castle.

Elsa, Anna, and Olaf ran to the window. There was a shadowy figure walking toward them!

"Stay here," Elsa said, running down the hall. But Anna and Olaf followed. They couldn't let Elsa face the Hairy Hooligan alone!

Elsa opened the castle door, and the friends peered into the darkness. Olaf held Anna's hand, bracing himself for the Hairy Hooligan's pointed teeth and sharp claws.

But it wasn't a monster after all. It was Sven!

"Sven!" Elsa called out. "What's wrong?"

Anna took one look at the reindeer and guessed what was going on. "You couldn't sleep, could you, Sven?" She patted him on the nose. "I bet Kristoff is snoring and keeping you awake. The trolls said his snores are loud enough to start an avalanche!"

Sven nodded.

"You should come to our sleepover!" Olaf said. "From what I can tell, there's very little sleeping involved."

Soon the group was happily settled in Elsa's room.

"How about another story?" Elsa suggested. She held up the book her parents had read to her and Anna all those years earlier.

"Excellent!" Anna agreed. She fluffed some pillows, and she, Olaf, and Sven got comfortable as Elsa began reading.

"'Once upon a time . . .'"

A little while later, Elsa reached her favorite part of the story.

"'And then the brave queen slayed the dragon,'" she read. Elsa stopped, hearing the sounds of heavy breathing around her. The rest of the slumber party had fallen asleep!

Smiling, Elsa put down the book. She gently tucked in Anna, Olaf, and Sven and climbed into bed.

Then, with one last look at Anna and her friends, Elsa, too, drifted off to sleep.

CHILDHOOD TIMES

It was a beautiful day in the little kingdom of Arendelle. King Agnarr and Queen Iduna proudly stood in the castle courtyard. The baron and baroness of Snoob had just arrived for a visit. If all went well, Arendelle would have a new partner in trade by the end of the trip.

Upstairs, Elsa and Anna stared in disbelief at their breakfast.

"We get chocolate just because there are some fancy visitors?" Anna asked.

"I suppose we *could* refuse to eat it," Elsa teased.

"No!" Anna chomped on her chocolate croissant. "Elsa, can we play with the magic?"

"We're supposed to stay in our rooms and not disturb the guests," Elsa said.

"Pleeeeease?" Anna begged. "We can hide. They won't see us!"

"Okay!" Elsa agreed. "Let's play. But we have to be very quiet."

Looking around to make sure they weren't spotted, the girls made their way to the kitchen. With a mischievous grin, Elsa made huge amounts of snow and ice. Soon the sisters were having a big snowball fight.

"See that pan?" Elsa shouted. She hit it with a flying snowball. "Woo-hoo!"

The two girls were having so much fun that they almost didn't see the king and queen arriving with their royal visitors! Quickly, Anna and Elsa slipped up the back staircase.

When the king and queen entered the kitchen, they were surprised to see all of the ice. But the royal visitors thought the snowballs were wonderful.

"Oh, my. This is just what we need on a warm summer's day!" exclaimed the baron. "You must try it, my dear!"

"Harumph!" The baroness stared at her bowl of ice.

"Ah, yes!" the king chuckled. "Ice is Arendelle's number one form of trade."

"Indeed! We harvest lots of ice from lakes up in the nearby mountains," the queen added.

As the king and queen spoke
with their guests, Anna and Elsa
played in the ballroom.

Suddenly, the girls heard the guests approaching.

"Uh-oh!" Elsa said, startled. "We'd better hide!"

"They almost saw us!" Anna chirped.

Giggling, the girls raced back to Elsa's room before they could get in trouble.

Downstairs, the king and queen entered the ballroom.
The king gasped when he saw the mounds of snow covering
the floor.

As the baroness stepped into the room, she slipped and
landed in a pile of snow.

"Oh, dear," the queen said. She and the king rushed to help.

"Snow angels!" the baroness cried, tossing snow into the air. "I love snow angels. What a delightful surprise!"

"I say," the baron chuckled. "The kingdom of Arendelle stops at nothing to please its visitors!"

After the visitors had gone to their guest rooms for the evening, the king and queen went to check on their daughters. They found the girls in Elsa's room. Both appeared to be sleeping soundly.

As the king and queen turned away, a small smile appeared on Anna's face.

As soon as the girls were alone, Anna popped upright.

"Elsa, do you want to play?" she asked.

"Anna, we can't! We're already going to be in a ton of trouble tomorrow," Elsa said.

Anna flopped back onto her pillow and sighed. "Still—"

"It was SO worth it!" the girls said together.

THE FROZEN MONSTER

It was a beautiful spring day in Arendelle. Queen Elsa was taking a break from her usual duties to spend time with her sister, Anna.

"Watch out!" Anna cried, speeding through the castle gates on her bike. The townspeople quickly jumped out of her way.

"That's not fair, Anna!" Elsa cried, racing after her sister. "You started before Olaf got to three!"

"First one to the harbor wins!" Anna yelled.

Behind the sisters, Olaf the snowman ran to catch up. "Wait for me!" he said. "Oooh . . . butterfly!"

Anna was almost to the harbor when a huge pile of snow appeared in front of her. She swerved to avoid it as Elsa rode past her, laughing.

"Elsa, using your powers is cheating!" Anna yelled.

"You're just jealous that I'm going to win!" Elsa called over her shoulder.

Just then, Elsa noticed Kristoff and Sven passing in front of her. They looked upset. She quickly stopped her bike to see what was wrong.

Anna raced past Sven, Kristoff, and Elsa. "Ha! Winner!" she called, hopping off her bike. Then she saw her friends' faces, and her smile disappeared. "Kristoff, are you okay?" she asked.

"We've been looking for you," Kristoff said. "Sven and I were gathering ice high in the mountains when we saw something huge in the forest! We tried to get a closer look, but the snow was blowing too hard, and we lost it. Elsa, can you control the snow so we can keep looking for it?"

"You have no idea what it was?" Elsa asked Kristoff.

"It looked like a monster, but I didn't get a good look at it. I thought I knew everything about those mountains, but I guess they can still surprise me!" Kristoff said.

"A new creature? Sounds like an adventure!" Anna said. "Oh! Can I name it?"

"Well, we'll have to find it first," Kristoff said.

The sisters hurried to the castle for supplies. On their way back to Kristoff and Sven, they ran into Olaf.

"Where'd you go?" the snowman asked. "I was right behind you, and then there was this butterfly, and . . ." Olaf looked at Anna's cloak. "What'd I miss?"

"We're going monster hunting!" Anna said.

"Oooh!" Olaf said. "Can I come?"

With Olaf in tow, the friends set out to find Sven and Kristoff's monster. The higher they climbed, the colder it became. Before long it began to snow . . . hard.

"Hey!" Olaf said, pointing at the snow falling on Elsa. "Now you have a snow cloud, too!"

Olaf happily grabbed Elsa's hands and began to dance with her. Elsa laughed and spun the little snowman around.

"Er, Elsa? A little help here?" Anna said.

Elsa turned to see her sister, Kristoff, and Sven freezing beneath a pile of snow. She quickly parted the storm to clear a path for her friends.

"Whew, that's better," Anna said, brushing herself off. "Now if only we could find our mysterious friend that easily."

"We've been walking for a long time," Elsa said a while later. "Are we almost to where you saw the monster, Kristoff?"

Kristoff and Sven looked at each other. "We . . . ahh . . . don't remember," Kristoff admitted.

"Don't remember!" the sisters said in unison.

"There was a lot of snow," Kristoff said, "and Sven took a wrong turn."

Sven groaned and nodded in agreement.

"How are we going to find the monster?" Anna asked.

Suddenly, a loud roar shook the mountain. Everyone froze.

"Wow, Sven. You sound hungry," Olaf said.

"I don't think that was Sven's stomach, Olaf. I think it was
the monster! Quick! Follow that roar!"
Anna cried.

The group started toward the noise. They hadn't gone far when they heard another roar coming from the opposite direction!

"Are there two of them?" Anna asked.

Elsa stopped and listened. "I think the roar is echoing off the rocks!" she said.

"So how do we find the monster?" Kristoff asked.

Elsa had an idea. She stomped her foot on the snow, and an icy staircase began to grow into the sky. Soon the stairs reached high above the trees. Now they would be able to see the whole forest!

"I never get tired of that," Kristoff said, admiring Elsa's icy creation.

Anna, Elsa, Kristoff, and Olaf began to climb the stairs. Below them, Sven whined. The steps were too slippery for him.

"I'll stay with you, Sven," Olaf said. "Besides, I think I'm afraid of heights!"

As Anna, Elsa, and Kristoff reached the top of the stairs, there was another great roar. "Look! The trees moved over there!" Anna pointed. "That must be where the monster is."

"You mean that patch of trees right next to us?" Kristoff asked.

"Yep!" Anna said.

Kristoff nodded. "Just checking."

At that moment, the trees moved again. The staircase shook. Sven ran behind the nearest tree, but Olaf had gotten distracted.

"Hello!" he said to a passing bird.

"Olaf, look out!" Anna cried. But it was too late. The mysterious monster crashed through the trees and stopped right in front of the snowman.

Olaf looked up. "It's Marshmallow!" he cried.

"Oh, right. Marshmallow! The giant ice monster who tried to attack us!" Kristoff said. "Shouldn't we be running right about now?"

Olaf gave Marshmallow a hug. "Marshmallow isn't scary! He's my friend!" Olaf looked up at the icy monster again. "How's my little buddy?" he cooed.

"He's right, Kristoff," Anna said as she started down the stairs. "Marshmallow doesn't look very scary anymore."

Marshmallow growled sadly. He sank to the ground and hugged Olaf closer.

"Wow, you're a really great hugger," Olaf said. "I think I'm being crushed."

Anna looked at Sven and Kristoff. Then she looked down at her hand, clasped tightly in her sister's.

"I think Marshmallow is lonely," Anna said.

Marshmallow nodded in agreement.

"I'm sorry, Marshmallow," Elsa said. "I thought you would be happy in the mountains. I guess I was wrong. I wish there was something we could do."

Sven and Kristoff looked at each other. They had an idea.

A few days later, Anna and Elsa were in the middle of a
rematch race when they spotted a giant figure near the harbor. It
was Marshmallow. He was helping Sven and Kristoff deliver ice!

"How's it going?" Anna asked Kristoff.

"Great! Just look how much more ice we've been able to
bring down the mountain!" Kristoff said.

Elsa smiled. "Marshmallow seems happy, too!"

Marshmallow nodded as he rubbed Sven's and Kristoff's
heads. He was glad to be part of the team!

ELSA'S GIFT

Snow fell quietly on Arendelle, blanketing the kingdom in white. The townspeople waded through deep snowdrifts. Snowflakes tickled children's noses and melted on their tongues. Everyone welcomed the snow, for this time it was not Queen Elsa's doing. It was winter!

Queen Elsa and Princess Anna watched from the castle window as their subjects prepared for the winter ball that evening.

Elsa smiled. For the first time since her childhood, the kingdom's gates were open. Her ice magic was under control. And most important, she and her sister were friends again.

Suddenly, Anna grabbed Elsa's arm and dragged her away from the window. "Come on!" she said. "We have so much to do to get ready for the ball!"

Elsa chuckled. Anna was right. There *was* still a lot to do!

Anna and Elsa had been working hard for days. Decorations hung from every wall, and the castle glittered with Elsa's frosty magic.

But there were still some final touches to add.

While Elsa finished icing the banquet room, Anna raced to the kitchen.

"There," she said, coming back with a tray full of *krumkake*. "The dessert table is ready! What do you think, Elsa?"

But Elsa wasn't paying attention.

"Earth to Elsa," Anna called.

Elsa looked at her sister and smiled. Anna's act of love had saved Arendelle—and Elsa. Elsa wanted to do something special to show everyone how much she loved her sister.

Glancing around the banquet room, Elsa had an idea. "I, um . . . I have to go," she told Anna.

Elsa raced out the door . . . and almost ran right into Olaf!

"Hi, Elsa," Olaf said. "Where are you going?"

"To the kitchen," Elsa said. "I'm going to make cookies for Anna. Do you want to help?"

Olaf clapped his hands. "I love cookies!"

The pair headed to the kitchen and locked themselves inside. They had just started getting ingredients together when Anna knocked on the door. "Elsa? Are you in there?" she called.

"Don't come in!" Elsa said. "You'll ruin the surprise!"

Elsa and Olaf waited until they heard Anna walk away. Then they finished gathering ingredients.

"You know," Elsa said to the snowman, "I don't think you should go anywhere near an oven."

"Pshaw!" Olaf exclaimed, waving his twiggy arms. "What could possibly go wrong?"

Soon the two were busy making extra-gingery gingerbread men—Anna's favorite. The cookies turned out perfectly, and Elsa only had to refreeze Olaf seven times!

Next Elsa decided to make Anna's favorite punch. She was stirring the punch when Anna walked into the kitchen.

"You can't be in here!" Elsa exclaimed. "I'm working on your surprise."

"I just want to—" Anna started, but Elsa cut her off.

"Just go to your room, Anna," Elsa said, turning her back on her sister. "I'll see you later."

Anna left, and Elsa finished making the punch. Then she went back to the ballroom. Everything looked beautiful, but there was nothing *special*. Elsa thought for a minute. Then, waving her hands, she created a glittering ice sculpture of Anna.

Just then, Kristoff came into the room. "I just saw Anna in the courtyard," he told Elsa. "She said you told her to go away! She seems upset."

"Oh, no! I didn't mean to hurt her feelings," Elsa said. "I just didn't want her to ruin her surprise!"

"You know, I think what she would really like is just to spend time with her big sister. You should go talk to her," Kristoff suggested.

"Thanks, Kristoff. I will!" Elsa said, running out of the room.

Elsa rushed into the snowy courtyard. "Anna? Where are
you?" she called, looking around. "Please come out. I'm so
sorry, Anna, I just—"

Splat! A snowball hit Elsa right in the face.

"Surprise!" Anna yelled, jumping out from behind a tree.

"W-what?" Elsa sputtered, brushing the snow off her face. "Did you just . . . ?"

Anna giggled. "It's a snowball intervention, Elsa," she said dramatically. "Since you don't have any time for me, I'm declaring war! I knew Kristoff could get you out here!"

Elsa started to grin. "Anna," she said. "I think you're forgetting which one of us has magical ice powers." She made a huge snowball and hurled it at Anna.

But Anna was ready for her. She had prepared a whole pile of snowballs!

The snowball fight went on and on, until at last Elsa called a truce. It was time for the sisters to get ready for the ball!

Elsa glanced slyly at Anna. Then, hurling one final snowball at her unsuspecting sister, she raced inside. "Gotcha!" she called over her shoulder.

That night, the sisters greeted their guests. As Anna looked around the banquet room, she noticed Elsa's cookies, her punch, and her beautiful ice sculpture.

"You did this for me?" Anna said.

Elsa nodded. "I wanted to give you the perfect gift."

"It's all lovely," Anna said. "And it was very sweet of you. But for me, the best present is just being with you."

"For me, too," Elsa said. And linking arms, the sisters went off to enjoy their party . . . together.

A New Friend

Spring had finally sprung in Arendelle. Olaf was enjoying the warm air when he saw Queen Elsa and Princess Anna coming toward him.

"Hi, Anna! Hi, Elsa!" he called. "Where are you going?"

Anna smiled at the snowman. "It's such a nice day, we thought we'd take a walk," she said. "Wanna come?"

Olaf couldn't believe his luck. A whole day with Anna and Elsa! Nodding, he hurried after the sisters.

The trio hadn't been walking long before they came upon
Wandering Oaken's Trading Post and Sauna.

"Ooh, a sauna!" Olaf said. "That sounds nice."

Anna giggled. "I'm not sure that's such a good idea," she
told the snowman. "But Oaken's store is always fun to look
around. Let's go say hi!"

Grabbing Elsa by the arm, Anna pulled her sister inside.

"Hoo-hoo!" called Oaken as the girls entered the trading post. "Big winter blowout sale!"

"Hi, Oaken!" Anna said. "Do you have anything special today?"

Oaken nodded. "These shoes for walking on snow are special. And that sled for sliding down mountains. Half off!"

Anna grinned. How could she say no to an offer like that?

Outside, Elsa looked at Anna. "I'm not sure any of that was exactly 'special,'" she said. "What are you going to do with all that winter gear in the middle of spring?"

Anna shrugged. "I'm sure I'll find some use for it," she said.

Olaf was looking over the supplies when a bumblebee buzzed past him. "Hello, bee," he said, and ran off after it.

Olaf followed the bee, and Anna and Elsa followed Olaf.
Soon they found themselves in a field of wildflowers.

"Oh, how pretty!" Anna said. She and Elsa began to pick
some flowers to bring home.

Meanwhile, Olaf chased after the bee. "Hey there, little
fella," he said. "Where are you—oof!"

"Olaf!" Anna cried. The snowman had
chased the bee right off a cliff!

"Hang on," Elsa said. Waving her hands, she
caught Olaf and pulled him back onto the cliff.

But Olaf wasn't paying attention to the sisters. He
was looking at a young reindeer stranded on the ledge
below him.

"You poor thing. How did you get down there?" Anna
asked. "And how are we going to get you up?"

"Hang on," Olaf called down. "We'll save you!" Then,
turning to Anna and Elsa, he said under his breath, "How are
we going to save him?"

Elsa thought for a moment. Then
she waved her hands, creating an
ice ramp for the reindeer to climb.
"Whoa," said Olaf,
admiring the ramp.

The reindeer carefully stepped onto the ramp . . . but
the ice was too slippery, and he fell down!

"Now what?" asked Elsa.

"I know!" Anna said. Grabbing her bag of winter gear, she slid down the ramp. "Hey, that was fun!" she said when she landed next to the reindeer.

Anna began to dig through her bag of supplies. She had a job to do!

First Anna put the
snowshoes on the reindeer's
hooves. Then she tied a rope around
the reindeer.

"See? I told you I'd find a use for this
stuff," she called up to Elsa.

Elsa grinned. "Okay, okay. You were right. Now what?"

Anna tossed the rope up to her sister. "Pull!"

Elsa and Olaf pulled with all their might. Finally, everyone was safely off the ledge.

The reindeer was so grateful he gave Olaf a big kiss.

"Awww, thanks, buddy," Olaf said. Then he turned to Anna and Elsa. "Can he come home with us?" he asked.

"Of course!" Elsa said with a smile. "And I know the fastest and most fun way for all of us to get home."

Elsa grabbed Anna's and Olaf's hands and led them to the sled.
"Hold on!" she cried. Then, using her magic,
she created a series of snow slides.
The trio zoomed down the
mountain with the reindeer
close behind.

The group slid gracefully through the castle gates and into the ballroom.

"Whee!" Anna cried.

"Can we do that again?" Olaf asked.

Elsa smiled at her friends and then looked at the reindeer. She was glad to be home. But she was even happier to have found a new friend.

Olaf's Birthday

"Elsa! Do you know what today is?" Anna asked, rushing into her sister's room.

Elsa laughed. "Should I?"

"One year ago today, you were crowned queen of Arendelle, milady." Anna curtsied dramatically.

"Aha!" Elsa said. "I guess that means about one year ago, you saved me."

The sisters got dressed and were headed to breakfast when they heard a soft humming. Their friend Olaf was walking down the hall, a jolly hop in his step.

"Oh, my goodness!" Elsa whispered. "That means it's been one year since I made Olaf."

"You mean . . . it's his birthday?" Anna asked.

The two looked at each other guiltily. They knew they had to do something special for the snowman. The question was . . . what?

Anna and Elsa walked into town, hoping to find the perfect birthday inspiration. Suddenly, Anna spotted a familiar face.

"Hoo-hoo!" called a tall blond man. He waved to the sisters from between a stall and a giant cart stacked high with supplies. Above the stall was a sign that read OAKEN'S WANDERING TRADING POST.

"Oaken!" Anna cried. "Do you have anything for birthdays?"

"You are in luck," Oaken said. "I have a new stock of balloons."

A few hours later, Anna and Elsa crept up a grassy hill,
holding some balloon strings tightly. They had told Olaf to
meet them there for a picnic and were planning on surprising
him with the balloons. After all, surprises were the best parts of
birthdays.

As soon as they were close to Olaf, the sisters yelled, "SURPRISE!"

"GAH!" Olaf jumped in shock, causing his arms and head to go flying off.

"Oh, no!" Elsa rushed over to reassemble him.

"Olaf!" Anna cried, reaching out to help.

When Olaf was back together again, he giggled. "What a great game," he said. "Now it's my turn: SURPRISE!" Olaf shouted at the sisters.

Anna and Elsa looked at one another. This would not do. They'd have to plan a different sort of birthday surprise.

Anna and Elsa said good-bye to Olaf and walked back to Oaken's.

"Hoo-hoo!" Oaken greeted them. "Big sale today. Tea cozies, two for one. Great deal, yah?"

"Actually, what about these?" Anna asked, eyeing what looked like a few musical instruments. She had an idea.

Soon Anna, Elsa, and their friend Kristoff were waiting for
Olaf at another one of the snowman's favorite spots: the shipping
docks. Kristoff was one of the best singers they knew, so Anna and
Elsa had asked him to lead them in a surprise birthday song.

When Olaf arrived, the group erupted into song. "Happy
birthday, Olaf!"

"Somebody else is named Olaf?" the little snowman asked
with glee. "I've got to go find him. He won't want to miss this
great song!" Olaf hurried off, leaving everyone behind in
stunned silence.

"Not to point out the obvious," Kristoff said, "but I think
the guest of honor just left."

Anna and Elsa looked at each other
again. *Now* what were they going to do?

Back at Oaken's, Anna and Elsa looked at the shelves.

"Ice-carving kits?" Oaken offered. "They are all the rage."

Anna giggled. "Well, I don't think we need one of those, right, Elsa? Elsa?"

But her older sister was looking at some bright orange candles.

"What's the one thing every birthday must have?" she asked Anna.

"CAKE!" they cried in unison.

Anna and Elsa spent the rest of the day baking a cake to go with their new festive candles.

"Oooooh!" Olaf said when he saw the lit candles. "Tiny fire!"

Sven also seemed very interested in the candles. He inched his way forward, sticking his snout closer and closer.

"I think Sven really likes tiny fire, too," Olaf observed.

"Uh-oh." Kristoff stepped in. "No, Sven, those aren't . . ."

". . . carrots!"

Kristoff finished his warning just as Sven tried to chomp on one of the candles. Startled, Anna and Elsa dropped the cake, lit candles and all, to the floor.

"Would you look at that," Olaf said. "Tiny fire makes big fire!"

Elsa hurried to freeze the flames while Kristoff and Anna held Sven and Olaf back. Another birthday surprise gone wrong. . . .

Feeling a bit defeated, Anna and Elsa headed back to Oaken's one last time.

"Hoo-hoo!" said the shop owner. "Evening special on tropical decorations."

The sisters looked at each other.

"That actually might be perfect," Anna said.

"Yes! A summer island party for Olaf!" Elsa declared.

"Happy birthday to you, Olaf!" Elsa announced that evening.

"It's my birthday?" Olaf grinned. "That must be why it's been the best day ever!"

"It has?" Anna asked.

"Of course! First you taught me that great surprise game at our picnic. Then I got to hear some music at the docks, and there was the fire show! And now this party!"

The sisters were amazed. Even though things hadn't gone as planned, Olaf had enjoyed all of their birthday surprises.

As Anna, Elsa, Kristoff, and Sven gave Olaf his birthday present—a nice, warm group hug—Olaf grinned.

"I just have one question," he declared.

"What's that?" Kristoff asked.

"What's a birthday?"

BABYSITTING THE TROLL TOTS

Anna, Kristoff, and Sven had special plans. They were babysitting the troll toddlers while Bulda and Grand Pabbie went to their annual magical prophesying convention.

"Kristoff! Sven! Anna! Welcome!" Bulda cried when they arrived. "We missed you!"

Bulda looked Kristoff over. "It seems like just yesterday you were young enough to need a sitter," she said.

"Remember when all he wanted to do was run naked through the valley?" Grand Pabbie asked.

"Oh, really?" Anna asked, stifling a giggle. "You never mentioned that."

"Okay, okay. That's enough stories for now," Kristoff groaned.

Bulda took Anna and Kristoff to the troll tots.

"If they get hungry, you can feed them smashed berries. And they may need a leaf change. But it's just about their bedtime, so they should be sleeping soon," she said.

As the adult trolls headed off, Anna waved. "Have a great time! Everything is going to be . . ."

". . . A DISASTER!" she finished.

The troll toddlers had escaped from their pen when no one was looking. Now they were running, climbing, and swinging all over the place.

"Oh . . . no, no," Anna said, rushing toward a group of trolls who were climbing massive boulders. "That's dangerous."

Kristoff ran over to a leaning tower of trolls that had sprouted.

"All right, guys," he said, gently pulling the trolls off one another. "Let's settle down now."

But the more Kristoff, Anna, and Sven tried to calm the little trolls, the wilder they became.

"Maybe they're hungry!" Anna said, heading for the basket of smashed berries.

"Yummy!" she cooed, offering one of the toddlers a spoonful of berries. But the trolls clearly felt they had better things to do.

"Maybe they need changing," Kristoff said. He peered into one of the trolls' nappy leaves. "Nope."

"Let's put them to bed," Anna suggested. "They must be tired by now."

But alas, the young trolls were wide-awake.

Suddenly, Anna heard a cheery voice.

"Hello, troll babies!"

It was Olaf!

"Elsa sent me in case you needed some help," Olaf
explained, turning to the clamoring trolls. "Why, hi, there.
Ha-ha! That tickles!"

"Boy, are we glad to see you," Kristoff said.

Anna ran to greet the snowman. But in her hurry, she tripped and fell face-first into the basket of berries! "Whoaaa!" Kristoff rushed to her side. "Anna! Are you okay?"

Anna lifted her head. Her face was covered in dripping purple goop.

The little trolls burst into loud giggles. They stampeded toward her and lapped up the berry juice on her cheeks.

Anna laughed. "Well, I guess that's *one* way to feed them."

When the trolls were done eating, they sat in a heap, happy and full. Suddenly, a strange smell floated through the air. The trolls looked down at their leaves.

"Uh-oh," Kristoff said knowingly. "Olaf, you distract them."

Olaf happily told the little trolls stories about his most favorite thing in the world: summer! Anna and Sven collected leaves while Kristoff changed diapers. Soon everyone was clean and sweet-smelling once more.

"And now for my showstopping song about summer!" Olaf announced.

Anna noticed that the trolls were swaying. Some of them were having trouble keeping their eyes open.

"Actually," she said, "maybe Kristoff and Sven would like to sing a lullaby instead."

As Anna and Olaf put the trolls to bed, Kristoff began to play his lute.

"Rock-a-bye, troll-ys, in your small pen," Kristoff sang.

"Time to go sleepy for Uncle Sven," he continued in Sven's voice.

By the time the adult trolls returned, the toddlers were
sound asleep.

"Wow, great job," Bulda whispered.

"It was easy," Anna replied, elbowing Kristoff.

"Piece of mud pie," Kristoff added.

Bulda smiled. "You two will be great parents someday!"

THE ICE GAMES

It was winter in Arendelle—the happiest winter in many years.

Princess Anna and Kristoff were inside, reading quietly in front of a roaring fire. Suddenly, the sound of children's laughter came through the open window. Anna put her book down and went to the window.

"Oh!" she said. "Come look, Kristoff. It's soooo cute!"

Kristoff joined Anna at the window. Three children were building a toboggan in the snowy courtyard below. Kristoff smiled at the children, but Anna could see that he was thinking about something else.

"All right," Anna said. "Out with it. What's on your mind?"

Kristoff turned to Anna. "I didn't have a lot of friends when
I was a kid," he said. "I mean, I had Sven. And the trolls. But only
humans are allowed to enter the Ice Games."

"The what?" Anna asked.

"Every year on the winter solstice, ice harvesters and their
families from all over the world gather on a glacier and hold the
Ice Games. It's supposed to be really fun. But you have to have a
three-person team." Kristoff looked a little sad. "I bet those kids
are building that toboggan for the big race. . . ."

Later Anna told Elsa what Kristoff had said. "It was so sad to hear him talk about missing the Ice Games," she said. "So I was thinking—"

"That we should take Kristoff to the games this year!" Elsa finished for her, delighted. "The three of us can be a team!"

"Yes!" Anna said, hugging her sister. "I knew you'd get it!"

Anna and Elsa quickly packed everything they would need
for the journey to the games. Then they ran to tell Kristoff about
their plan.

"You'd do that for me?" he asked, his face red.

"Of course!" Anna said cheerfully. "Every ice harvester
should get to go to the Ice Games!"

The day before the winter solstice, Anna, Elsa, and Kristoff arrived at the Ice Games. Anna couldn't help staring at the group around her. She'd never seen so many ice harvesters in one place!

"Say," one of them said, pointing at Elsa, "isn't that the queen of Arendelle? I heard she has magic ice powers."

"No fair!" said another. "She'll use her powers to win the games!"

"I promise on my honor as queen that I will not use my powers in the games," Elsa said solemnly.

"Yeah, so back off," said a gruff voice. Anna turned to see a group of ice harvesters from Arendelle standing behind her. With them were the three children she had seen outside the palace window! Anna grinned. She loved that the people of Arendelle were so loyal to her sister.

"Our queen wouldn't cheat," the little girl from Arendelle said. "And she doesn't need to, anyhow."

It was true: Elsa didn't need to use her powers to win the first contest. She carved a gorgeous ice statue of the rock trolls using just a hammer and a chisel.

Next was Anna and Kristoff's event.

"I don't care what the event is. I know we're going to win!" Anna said.

"Couples ice-skating," the announcer boomed.

"Unless it's that . . ." Anna said, her heart sinking. She was a terrible ice-skater.

But Anna wasn't one to back down from a challenge. She and Kristoff gave it their all, swooping and speeding around the rink. Kristoff managed a little jump, and Anna only fell down nine times. They didn't win, but they had a lot of fun trying . . . and they did manage to come in third place.

That night Anna, Elsa, and Kristoff had dinner with the rest of the ice harvesters. As they ate, they discussed the Ice Games.

"With Elsa's first-place finish, and Kristoff and me coming in third in the ice-skating," Anna said, "we actually stand a chance of winning the Ice Games!"

"All we have to do is win the big toboggan race tomorrow," Kristoff agreed.

"Good luck!" Anna heard a small voice behind her say. She turned around to see the little girl from Arendelle.

"Thank you," Anna replied with a smile. "You made the ice sculpture of the palace today, right?"

The girl nodded, blushing furiously.

"It was beautiful," Elsa said. "And I know a little something about making ice palaces!"

Grinning from ear to ear, the little girl ran back to sit with her family.

"Good luck to you, too!" Anna called after her.

"What a sweet little girl," Elsa said. "She reminds me of someone else at her age."

"Me?" Anna asked hopefully.

"I said 'sweet,' Anna. Not 'annoying,'" Elsa replied with a wink.

Anna punched her sister playfully.

"Of course, I meant you, Anna," Elsa admitted.

"One more round of hot chocolate?" Kristoff suggested.

"Yes, please!" Anna and Elsa said together.

As the sun rose the next morning, Anna, Elsa, and Kristoff piled into their toboggan. It was time for the last event.

"Here we gooooooo!" Anna shrieked. The trio rocketed down the slope with the rest of the racers.

Anna squinted against the wind as their toboggan went faster and faster. Soon they had pulled ahead of the other racers. "We're winning!" she yelled.

Anna, Elsa, and Kristoff were almost to the finish line
when another toboggan passed them. It was moving so fast they
couldn't even see who was inside.

The toboggan streaked down the slope and across the finish
line. It was the children from Arendelle!

"We won! We won!" the kids yelled, hugging each other and
jumping up and down. Watching them celebrate, Anna couldn't
bring herself to be disappointed that she, Kristoff, and Elsa
hadn't won.

She just hoped Kristoff wasn't too upset.

"I'm sorry we didn't come in first, Kristoff," Elsa said later, as they took their place on the winners' podium.

Kristoff grinned. "Nah," he said. "Don't be. I finally got to compete in the Ice Games! And I think it's great that they won. Having friends you can count on is really important when you're a kid."

Anna hugged Kristoff. "Having friends you can count on is really important forever. And I have the best friends of all!"

ACROSS THE SEA

Anna and Elsa were going on a trip to visit some neighboring kingdoms. As they climbed aboard their ship, the captain scurried over.

"Your Majesty," he said to Elsa. "I don't think we'll make it to our first stop on time. Not with waters this still."

"Don't worry," Anna said, taking the wheel.

"We've got it covered," Elsa said, creating a light snow flurry to push them along.

Soon the ship arrived at its first port: the kingdom of Zaria.

"Welcome, Queen Elsa and Princess Anna!" King Stebor called in a booming voice.

"We cannot wait to show you our kingdom," Queen Renalia added warmly.

First the king and queen of Zaria invited the sisters to lunch, where Anna and Elsa enjoyed tasty new foods. Then the queen took Anna and Elsa on a tour of her prized gardens. The sisters had never seen so many amazing flowers!

That night, the girls were treated to a grand festival.

"We've heard so much about your special talents," Queen Renalia said to Elsa. "Won't you show us some of your magic?"

Suddenly, Elsa felt very shy. She nodded at the dance floor.

"Would you like to join the dancing, Your Majesties?" she asked, changing the subject. "That looks like fun."

The next stop on Anna and Elsa's tour was a kingdom called Chatho. The sisters met Chatho's ruler, Queen Colisa, in front of her impressive palace.

"Thank you for having us, Your Majesty," Elsa said.

"Of course," the queen responded. "I am very happy you are both here!"

Queen Colisa first took the sisters on a walk through the kingdom's rain forest, where they saw many unique animals.

Anna was particularly fond of some bashful furry creatures. "Why, hello there!" she said, waving at the animals.

After their walk, the queen led Anna and Elsa into an enormous gallery. Chatho was known for its striking art and relics.

As Anna admired Chatho's treasures, Elsa spoke with the queen. "These are beautiful," she said.

"I'm so glad you think so," Queen Colisa replied. "Would you like to add a sculpture to our collection?"

Suddenly, Elsa noticed a block of ice under a spotlight, ready to be carved. Once again, she felt a wave of shyness.

Noticing her sister's discomfort, Anna jumped in. "Um . . . sure! Ice sculptures are actually my specialty!"

Later, as they got off their ship in the next kingdom, Anna asked Elsa why she didn't want to show off her powers.

"I guess I just got nervous," Elsa admitted.

Anna was about to reply when she spotted someone surprising: the Duke of Weselton!

"What are *you* doing here?" Anna asked. The sisters had purposefully avoided Weselton on their tour. Their final stop was the kingdom of Vakretta, far from the Duke's home.

The Duke smoothed his coat. "I am visiting my mother's cousin's wife's nephew, if you must know. Although I wish I weren't. If I were you, I would turn my ship around right now."

The sisters looked at each other.

The Duke sighed. "Vakretta is having the hottest summer in years. Of course, you wouldn't care about *that*."

As the sisters followed the Duke into the village, they noticed Vakrettans sprawled out, sweaty and tired.

"Whoa," Anna remarked.

For once, Elsa didn't feel shy. She knew she had to do something to cool the people down. She quickly conjured some snow clouds, much to the delight of the villagers.

"It's working!" the Duke cried in surprise.

Elsa started making frosted mugs out of ice. "Why don't you
get us some lemonade?" she asked.

Soon Vakretta was a frozen wonderland.
The citizens ice-skated and built beautiful snow castles.

"I suppose a thank-you is in order," the Duke said
begrudgingly. "I frankly don't know where to begin. . . ."

"Well, you could grab a board," Elsa suggested, winking at Anna.

The Duke turned red and started sputtering. "A duke would
never . . . it isn't . . ."

"It's okay. We'll show you how it's done," Anna called as she and
Elsa grabbed some planks and slid down a hill.

THE MIDSUMMER PARADE

It was a beautiful summer day. The breeze was soft, the sun was warm, and birds were singing happily. Elsa and Anna were picking wildflowers in a field not far from town.

"I can't believe it'll be midsummer soon," Anna said, looking around the lush green meadow.

Elsa grinned. "I love midsummer," she said. "Remember when we were kids and I used to lead—"

"The midsummer parade!" Anna interrupted, finishing her sister's sentence. The midsummer parade was one of her happiest childhood memories.

"I *loved* that parade," Anna told her sister. "You always looked so fancy, riding at the head of it."

"On that fat little pony," Elsa said with a chuckle. "Mister Waffles."

"We haven't had a midsummer parade since we were little kids," Anna said sadly.

Elsa nodded. "Now that the gates are open, we should have it again. Starting this year!"

Anna clapped her hands. "You'll look so great at the head of the parade," she told her sister.

Elsa grinned slyly. "Not me. *You!* I hereby declare you Midsummer Princess."

Anna, Elsa, and their friends started planning the parade the very next day.

"Marching band?" Elsa said.

"Already rehearsing," Kristoff said.

"Flowers?" Anna asked.

"I've been collecting them all—*achooo!*—week!" Olaf said, sniffling.

Anna consulted the parade planning checklist. "Next up, clothing!"

Anna and Elsa went to search the royal wardrobe.

"How about this?" Anna asked, putting a silly hat on Elsa.

Elsa giggled and held up some boots. "These are definitely you," she told Anna.

The sisters picked wilder and wilder outfits for each other. Soon they were laughing so hard they could hardly stand.

"Okay, it's time to get serious," Elsa said. "You need something special to wear to the parade!"

With a little help from Anna's friends, the parade was shaping up beautifully. It was going to be exactly like when Anna and Elsa were kids! Well . . . almost exactly.

"I don't think you can ride Mister Waffles in the parade," Elsa told Anna. "You're bigger than he is now. Besides, I'm pretty sure he's retired."

"Then I'll have to find a new horse!" Anna said. "The best horse in all of Arendelle."

Anna and Olaf headed to the stable to find the right horse. "What about that one?" Anna asked the head groom, pointing at an elegant mare.

"She's so pretty!" Olaf sighed admiringly.

"This is Lady Crystalbrook Shinytoes the Fourth," the head groom said.

Lady Crystalbrook Shinytoes the Fourth stepped toward Anna . . . and tripped over her own feet. She fell right into the pond!

"Oh, dear," Anna said.

"How about him?" Olaf asked, pointing at a big, strong horse. "What's his name?"

The groom cleared his throat. "Dauntless."

"Hello, Dauntless," Anna said sweetly. As she stepped forward to pet the horse, a leaf fluttered by in the wind. When Dauntless saw the leaf, his eyes widened. With a loud, frightened whinny, he turned and ran away as fast as he could.

"I do *not* think you should ride *him*," Olaf said.

Anna thought the third horse looked very promising . . . until he tried to eat Olaf's nose!

"Hey!" Olaf giggled. "That tickles!"

Hours later, Anna was at her wit's end. They had met *every* horse, but they hadn't found the right one. "I don't know what to do," she said miserably. "Maybe we should just cancel the parade."

"Cancel the parade?"

Anna and Olaf looked up to find Kristoff entering the stable. "Why would you do that?" he asked.

"I can't find the right horse to lead the parade," Anna said.

"Hmmm," Kristoff said. "I think I know just the fellow for the job."

"You do?" Olaf said. "Who's the horse?"

"Well . . ." Kristoff said, "he isn't exactly a *horse*."

"Sven," Kristoff said, slinging his arm around the reindeer's shoulders, "how would you like to lead the parade?"

"Gee whiz," Kristoff said in Sven's voice, speaking for his friend, "I'd be delighted!" And Sven *did* look delighted.

"Oh," Anna said, clasping her hands happily, "Sven is *perfect*!
He's loyal, and brave, and smart!"

"And handsome," Kristoff added in his Sven voice.

"And handsome," Anna agreed. She kissed Sven's nose.

Anna introduced Sven to the royal stables' grooms. "He's
going to be leading the parade with me," she explained. "So he
needs to look extra fancy."

"It's an honor," the head groom said, bowing low. "Please
come with us, sir."

The grooms set to work on Sven. They oiled his hooves.
They polished his antlers. And they brushed and brushed and
brushed his fur.

When the royal grooms were done with Sven, he positively shone!

"Sven," Anna said, "you look Svendid!" She elbowed Elsa. "Get it? *Sven*did?"

"I get it," Elsa said with a smile. "You really do look magnificent, Sven." Then she frowned. "But I think there's something missing."

Elsa hung a huge flower wreath around Sven's neck.

"There," she said. "Now you're perfect."

Anna looked at the checklist. "Band, flowers, Sven . . . I think everything's ready," she said.

Olaf jumped up and down in excitement. "It's parade time!" he cried.

The birds sang, the band played, and the people of
Arendelle cheered as the parade wound its way through town.
Anna was so happy she couldn't stop smiling.
The midsummer parade was perfect.

Later Anna and Elsa celebrated the successful parade. "We did it, Anna!" Elsa said. "The parade was just like when we were kids!"

"No," Anna said, grinning at her sister. "It was even better."

OLAF'S PERFECT SUMMER DAY

Summer had arrived in Arendelle. Everyone was enjoying the long, sunny days after a very cold winter.

This was going to be the hottest day of the year! Most of the villagers wanted to stay inside, where it was cool . . . but Olaf could hardly wait to get outside! This was the kind of day he had always dreamed of!

"Anna! Anna!" Olaf called, running into the princess's room. "Guess what today is? It's the perfect summer day! Let's go outside and play. I bet there will be bees buzzing and dandelions fuzzing everywhere!"

Anna groaned as she sat up in bed. It was sure to be hot and sticky outside! Then she saw Olaf's hopeful face. How could she say no?

Anna got dressed, and the two went to look for Elsa.

"There you are!" Olaf cried joyfully when they found her at last. "Today is exactly the kind of day I've been waiting for my whole snowman life. Please, can we go play in the sunshine?"

Elsa laughed. "That sounds like fun, Olaf," she said.

Olaf, Anna, and Elsa set off at once for their fun summer day. In the royal gardens, they noticed some children lying on the grass. Giggling, Olaf ran up to them.

"Hi, my name is Olaf. Don't you just love summer?"

The children were so charmed by Olaf that they jumped up and began to tumble about.

Soon Olaf had all the children chasing butterflies and blowing fuzz off dandelions. Summer was exactly like he'd always imagined!

After a little while, Anna plopped down on the grass. "Whew! All that running tired me out!" she said.

Elsa agreed. "Let's head to the docks. I think we can find a nice boat to sail to the fjord."

Olaf, who had been chasing a bumblebee, stopped in his tracks. "We're going sailing? I've always wanted to try sailing!"

At the docks, Anna and Elsa chose a beautiful sailboat. As
they set sail, Olaf hummed happily. He even got to steer the boat!

When they reached the shore, Anna set up a picnic. But Olaf couldn't sit still. "Don't you just love the feeling of sand on your snow, Anna?" he squealed.

Anna gingerly stuck her toe in the sand. "Oh, goodness, that is . . . uh . . . warm," she squeaked.

Anna ran to cool her feet in the water. Meanwhile, Olaf chased the waves . . . and was chased *by* them!

The three friends spent the whole afternoon playing in the summer sun.

They built sand castles and sand people, and they even danced with the seagulls!

Finally, when they'd tired themselves out, Anna, Elsa, and Olaf had a picnic on the shores of the fjord.

"Hands down, this is the best day of my life," said Olaf.

As they sailed back to Arendelle, Olaf admired the beautiful colors the setting sun made in the sky. "I wish I could hug the summer sun," he said. "I bet it would feel wonderful!"

Anna smiled tiredly. "You might need a bigger snow flurry for that, Olaf," she said.

Back at the docks, Kristoff and Sven had just returned from harvesting the mountain lakes. Now their sled was full of ice. Jumping out of the boat, Anna flung herself against the deliciously cold blocks. "Oh, am I glad to see you!" she exclaimed.

Meanwhile, Olaf told Kristoff and Sven all about his adventures. When he finished, he sighed with happiness. "I wish it could always be summer!" he said.

Elsa smiled mischievously. "Summer is
pretty wonderful. But tomorrow, I predict a
chance of snow."